FREE LUNCH

WRITTEN BY
J. OTTO SEIBOLD
and
VIVIAN WALSH

ILLUSTRATED BY
J. OTTO SEIBOLD

VIKING

VIKING
Published by the Penguin Group
Penguin Books USA Inc., 375 Hudson Street, New York, New York 10014, U.S.A.
Penguin Books Ltd, 27 Wrights Lane, London W8 5TZ, England
Penguin Books Australia Ltd, Ringwood, Victoria, Australia
Penguin Books Canada Ltd, 10 Alcorn Avenue, Toronto, Ontario, Canada M4V 3B2
Penguin Books (N.Z.) Ltd, 182-190 Wairau Road, Auckland 10, New Zealand

Penguin Books Ltd, Registered Offices: Harmondsworth, Middlesex, England

First published in 1996 by Viking, a division of Penguin Books USA Inc.

10 9 8 7 6 5 4 3 2 1

LIBRARY OF CONGRESS CATALOGING-IN-PUBLICATION DATA
Seibold, J.otto.
Free lunch / by J.otto Seibold and Vivian Walsh ; illustrated by J.otto Seibold
p.   cm.
Summary : When a bad elephant takes over the bird seed company,
Mr. Lunch tries to find a better source of food for his feathered friends.
ISBN 0-670-86988-0 (hardcover)
[1. Dogs—Fiction.   2. Birds—Fiction.   3. Elephants—Fiction.   4. Animals—Fiction.]
I. Walsh, Vivian.   II. Title.
PZ7.S45513Fr 1996 [E]—dc20   96-15253 CIP AC

Printed in U.S.A.
Set in Times and Arbitrary Bold

MR. LUNCH

dedicated
TO NEd
and
gunild

lunch

night
time

morning

sleeping

WAS **VERY** g**OOD AT**

CHASING BIRDS

IN FACT, HE WAS

A PROFESSIONAL

our

story

begins...

Every morning Mr. Lunch liked to meet with the
birds for bird-chasing practice. To get ready to go
really fast, Mr. Lunch would stre-e-etch his back, and
the birds would flap their wings:

One—two   One—two.
One—two   three—four.

Afternoons were reserved for office work. There
was a lot to do, such as reading the mail and placing
bird seed orders.

One afternoon, Mr. Lunch got a letter from the Elephant Brand Bird Seed Company. It said there was a new elephant in charge.

The old president was a good elephant with an excellent nose for seeds.

Mr. Lunch wondered where he could have gone. Maybe the elephant went on one of his trips, thought Mr. Lunch.

Mr. Lunch was happy to order some new seeds from the new elephant.

But the new seeds did not make the birds happy.
As time passed the seeds became . . .

WORSE,

WORSE,

ROCKS.

The matter was brought to Mr. Lunch's attention. He conducted a careful examination and determined that the seeds were, indeed, rocks.

The birds didn't like rocks.

Ambrose, the red bird, said, "I have an idea."

He had a friend who lived in the country, surrounded by birdseed trees.

"Maybe we should go visit," said Ambrose.

Everybody liked Ambrose's idea.

RAKE

WHEELBARROW

FIELD GUIDE

GLOVES

BASKETS

LADDER

SNACK

BOOT

They gathered everything they would need to pick the seeds,

and then drove off to find Ambrose's friend.

Ambrose was happy to see his old friend. Her
name was Gunhild. She showed them a good place
to get started.

It was a lovely garden.

But not everyone was so happy. High overhead,
someone was spying on them.

It was the new Bird Seed Company elephant.
He was very angry.
He did not like to see birds eating free seeds.
He did not like many things.
He did not like Mr. Lunch.
He hatched an evil elephant idea.
Quickly, he painted a sign. It read:

DOGS MUST REMAIN ON LEASH

Minutes later the police arrived and arrested Mr. Lunch for being off the leash.

Ambrose told the police they were making a big mistake.

"That's for the judge to decide," said the officer. "I should probably arrest you too, but I don't have a jail small enough to hold birds."

Mr. Lunch was sure there had been a misunderstanding. He didn't even have a leash. He would explain his story to the judge, and be set free.

But the judge was an owl. And like all owls, she stayed up all night, and slept all day. The judge never heard a word Mr. Lunch said. She was deep in sleep.

Mr. Lunch would have to wait in jail.

Mr. Lunch had never been in jail before.

ALIA

ELEPHANT

POPCORN

PHONE

mini

CATERPILLAR

LOCOMOTIVE

BABY

MONKEY

BEAR

Mr. Lunch spent his days looking for shapes in the clouds.

The nights were more lonely.

Ambrose wanted to help Mr. Lunch. It was time to pay a visit to the bake shop.

He asked the chef if he could hide something special inside a piece of cake. The chef said no-no, that would not be right, that would be breaking the Baker's Code.

He did have a little secret though, one that could help Mr. Lunch.

A pink package was prepared. Ambrose and Gunhild delivered it to jail.

Mr. Lunch was surprised when a piece of cake showed up. He ate it very carefully. He didn't want to swallow a file, or anything.

Mr. Lunch finished the cake without finding anything that could help him escape. He felt sad, but being a neat dog he still took care to wipe his face. As he was cleaning around his eyes, he noticed that there was some writing on his napkin. It was a map. Ambrose had drawn an escape route!

It turned out Mr. Lunch's jail room was right over an abandoned ruby mine.

Mr. Lunch began to dig...

He dug until he found a big surprise.

It was the ex-president of the Elephant Brand Bird Seed Company!

And he was surrounded by shiny red rocks...rubies!

Even though he was upside down Mr. Lunch could see the elephant was feeling sad and blue.

This was not on Ambrose's escape map. Mr. Lunch decided to investigate.

The elephant was mumbling. As Mr. Lunch got closer he heard, "Tricked, trapped, trick-trap, tripped.

"I have been tricked into a trap," said the elephant.

He told Mr. Lunch how the evil elephant had locked him up in the ruby mine so he could take over the Bird Seed Company.

Mr. Lunch knew this was true because he had been tricked by that elephant too.

The evil elephant had sealed the mine with a big rock. There was only one chance for escape. A hole in the ceiling. But, it was too small for an elephant, and too high up for a dog.

Things looked grim.

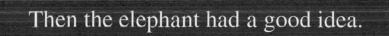
Then the elephant had a good idea.

Mr. Lunch shot through the roof and out
into the nighttime sky. He was free.

Far off in a tree Judge Owl was wide awake. She thought the flying dog looked familiar. As if from a dream.

She flew over to investigate.

As the owl and Mr. Lunch floated down to earth, Mr. Lunch explained everything. About the good elephant and the bad elephant, about the rubies and the rocks.

Judge Owl said, "Don't worry, I will take care of everything."

And she did.
When the good elephant saw that
his umbrella was broken he took the
pieces and made a
hat. Then he added
a single ruby to
remind him of his
time alone.

RUBY
ABANDONED
MINE

KEEP
OUT

5

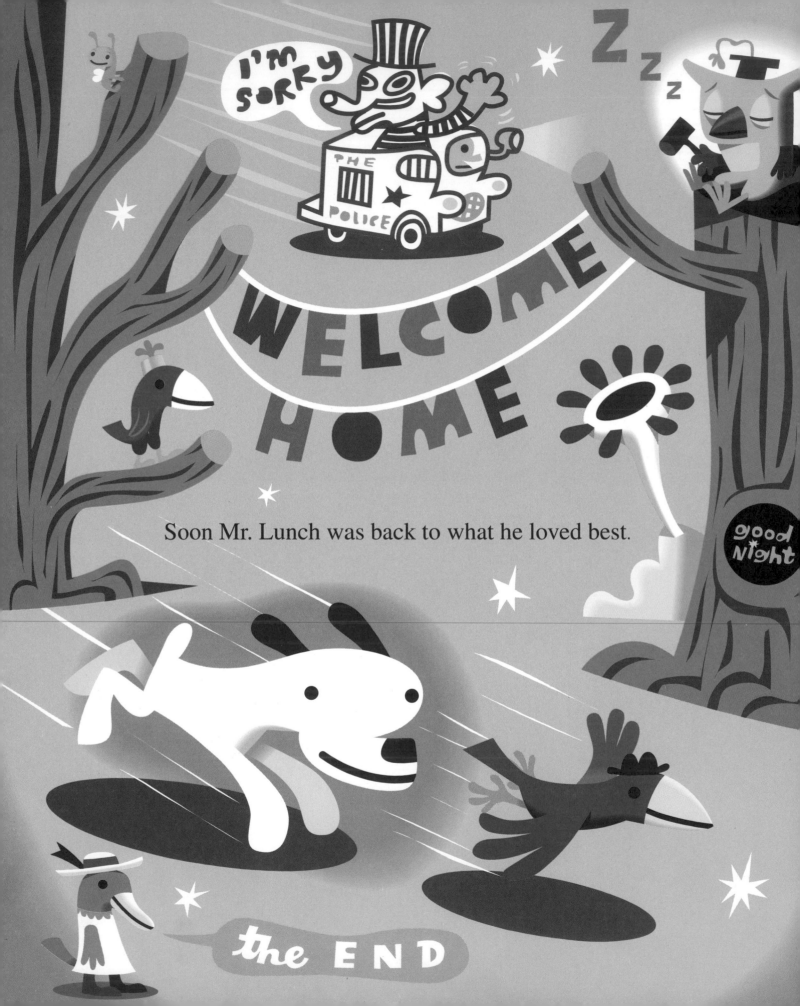

Soon Mr. Lunch was back to what he loved best.